I0708772

Carrie's Gift

Books by Michael Lister

(Love Stories)
Carrie's Gift

(John Jordan novels)
Power in the Blood
Blood of the Lamb
Flesh and Blood
The Body and the Blood
Blood Sacrifice

(Short Story Collections)
North Florida Noir
Florida Heat Wave
Delta Blues
Another Quiet Night in Desparation

(Remington James novels)
Double Exposure

(Merrick McKnight novels)
Thunder Beach
Spring Break

(Jimmy "Soldier" Riley novels)
The Big Goodbye
The Big Beyond

(Sam Michaels and Daniel Davis Series)
Burnt Offerings
Separation Anxiety

(The Meaning Series)
The Meaning of Jesus
Meaning Every Moment
The Meaning of Life in Movies

Carrie's Gift

Michael Lister

a love story

You buy a book. We plant a tree.

Inquiries should be addressed to:
Pulpwood Press
P.O. Box 35038
Panama City, FL 32412

Lister, Michael.
Carrie's Gift/ Michael
Lister.
-----1st ed.
p. cm.

ISBN: 978-1-888146-31-8 Hardcover

ISBN: 978-1-888146-32-5 Paperback

Library of Congress Control Number:

Book Design by Adam Ake

Printed in the United States

1 3 5 7 9 10 8 6 4 2

First Edition

For Amy Moore-Benson
a truly amazing gift to me!
What Emerson said is so very true of you.

The greatest gift is a portion of thyself.
Ralph Waldo Emerson

Thank You
Pam, Jill, Amy, Anitra, Adam

One

The classic Christmas carol playing desultorily through the rear speakers of the Shelby's superior sound system dies abruptly as I turn off the car in front of the brick facade of Kent Cannon Funeral Home and remove the keys as if I'm actually going to get out.

Unbuckling, I sit uncomfortably in the black-and-gray leather seat, my suit coat and overcoat bunched awkwardly around me.

I am here for the funeral of a classmate from a lifetime ago, and as I sit here perfectly still, a piece of a poem my eleventh grade lit teacher made me memorize drifts up from my subconscious like bits of dust floating in a random shaft of afternoon sunlight.

> Because I could not stop for Death
> He kindly stopped for me;
> The carriage held but just Ourselves
> And Immortality.

We're all stopping, aren't we? Stopping for death, for the funeral. Stopping because we can't not. But we're not the only ones who should. Everyone should stop for her, for this. And not just everyone, but no less than the wide world entire should stop its spin upon its axis.

In the way that way leads to way, the dab of Dickinson and the thought it inspires leads to a fragment of Auden.

> He was my North, my South, my East and West,
> My working week and my Sunday rest,
> My noon, my midnight, my talk, my song;
> I thought that love would last for ever: I was wrong.

> The stars are not wanted now: put out every one;
> Pack up the moon and dismantle the sun;
> Pour away the ocean and sweep up the wood.
> For nothing now can ever come to any good.

I am here for a funeral, true, and to do the eulogy, and to comfort and support my friends, my former classmates, but I am here mostly for Carrie—have come early in hopes of spending time alone with her.

The late December day is disconcerting—bright, clear, and sunny, but frigid as fuck with a brisk breeze that blows through the body and brings tears to the eyes—in its way, a metaphor for the incongruous and self-contradictory nature of North Florida itself.

As the temperature in the car drops, flashes of high school dances on cold nights following home football games fire in my memory and imagination—the cleared cafeteria floor sparkling with a thousand dots of light beneath the disco ball, tight, straight-leg jeans, narrow leather ties, huge combs hanging precariously out of back pockets, at the ready for quick retrieval to glide through feathered bangs, and slow dancing to sweet, uncynical love songs sung by earnest adults who seemed somehow to have written down our raw emotion for the sole purpose of singing it back to us.

My eyes are moist as I make myself lurch out of the car, and the cold wind blows tears onto my face.

I falter unsteadily toward the front door, finding each step far more difficult than the one before.

How am I going to get through this?

Uncertain what to expect, I pull open the large wooden door and step into the stifling heat of the lobby.

Death Incorporated.

As personal as a furniture store showroom, the large, lush lobby is filled with faux antique furniture, serene scenic paintings, and silk arrangements, an enormous gaudy gold chandelier dangling above it all.

The hushed hum of the milling mourners is maddening, their very presence irritating, intrusive, profane, but far worse is the occasional voice, or worse yet burst of laughter, that rises above the dull din.

Avoiding eye contact, I make my way over to the black plastic display board with the white snap-on letters, appalled that this is the best they can do for her.

Locating her name—one among five—my blurry vision follows the dots over to the visitation parlor's name. She's not in the Magnolia or the Orchid, but in the Rose Room.

Anger.

One among five. Assigned a little room like all the rest. And not just any room. The fuckin' Rose Room. Rose. The place couldn't be more trite if it tried.

Now I realize why I don't recognize anyone. These aren't her mourners, not our classmates and friends and community. This present group is here to grieve for another—what was the name above hers? Jay Bryan, Jr.— and should have mourned and moved on by the time the next group arrives.

Irrationally, irritably, I begrudge them their grief, and feel they are encroaching on mine. Whoever this Jay Bryan, Jr. is and however he died is irrelevant. He should've waited, they should've waited. She should not be one among many, should not be shoved in between Jay Bryan, Jr. and Cathryn K. Minton.

Their presence—these mourners and those to follow and those they come to mourn—diminishes everything somehow, detracts, defiles, and as I stumble down the broad, overly decorated corridor toward the Rose Room I want them gone, want them to take their pathetic grief and just go.

Is anything worse than a funeral at Christmas? I overhear someone say.

Yeah, I think. Dying at Christmas. Though I guess it depends, doesn't it, on what happens next.

Trembling—from what parts irrational anger and claustrophobia and soul-sick sadness I don't know—I shuffle as if to the tepid, tinny music dripping from the small ceiling-mounted speakers, passing beneath a series of smaller chandeliers, from door to door. All of them closed.

The wide hallway, with its polished claw-footed furniture and tasteless framed paintings, reminds me of a melodramatic depiction of the afterlife in a movie-of-the-week dream sequence, the closed doors various eternal choices.

This is all so surreal.

Just get in the room.

You think it'll be any better in there?

Two

Opening the door and seeing Carrie standing near the closed coffin, I get my answer.

She's here. Everything will be okay. Or at least better than I expected. She'll help me get through this.

Walking up and standing beside her, I remain silent for a moment. The family flowers on top of the casket contain a letter—one I wrote. She is reading it. Surprised and a little embarrassed to discover my personal letter on public display, I start to step back to take a seat in one of the chairs along the front row, but she turns and hugs me.

Ethan, she says. Oh my God I'm so glad you're here.

We hold each other for a long moment, our bodies

pressing hard against each other.

Is that the same scent she wore in school? Can't be, can it? Why do I think it is? Has my mind replaced the old olfactory memory with this new one?

Still striking, her simple black dress compliments her dark features—deep brown eyes, cinnamon skin, and thick, burnished black hair with a hint of auburn.

As we release one another, she says, Do funerals make you want to fuck, or is it just me?

I laugh. That's the Carrie I recall from so long ago, and the faint familiarity makes me miss not only her but all my classmates and our youth.

I'm serious. I'm horny as hell.

It's not just you. And I don't think it's just us. I bet most everybody wants to do some life-affirming something after a funeral—eat, fuck . . .

That all you got? Eat, fuck?

Ah . . . oh, anything creative—build something, make something, start something, experience some art.

After?

Huh?

You said after. How about during?

I smile. That a proposition?

Nice letter, she says, forcing a change of subject. You've always had a way with words. Remember that piece you wrote in honor of our twentieth reunion? They printed it in the bulletin with the obituary. I've always loved it so much. In this context it's like an obit for our class, our youth.

She hands it to me and I stumble back and sit down

to read it as she returns to the letter on the coffin.

It's been a few years since I wrote it, and I read it now not as its author, but as a member of the group it was written for.

Time After Time

This year, the Tupelo High School Class of 1986, of which I am a part, celebrates its twenty-year class reunion. 2006 is the twentieth year of our adulthood—we've now been out of school longer than we were in, many of us have children of our own about to graduate, and we've reached what is quite likely the halfway point of our lives. I find all this singularly sobering.

The year we graduated from high school, The Cosby Show was the top rated TV show; the number one song was That's What Friends Are For by Dionne Warwick and friends; It by Stephen King was the best-selling book; Lonesome Dove by Larry McMurtry won the Pulitzer Prize for fiction; and Out of Africa won Best Picture Oscar.

We came of age during the Reagan Years, when Wall Street's Gordon Gekko told us that greed was good, and the trickle-down effect of Reaganomics never quite reached us. We were the first group to be introduced to the PC, the CD, MADD, AIDS, MTV, ET, CNN, and DNA fingerprinting. Michael Jackson was the King of Pop and Oprah Winfrey was just beginning her reign as the Queen of TV.

Fashion was influenced by the dance clothes of movies like Fame and Flashdance and the music videos on

MTV—ripped sweatshirts, headbands, and who can ever forget leg warmers? Calvin Klein and Ralph Lauren were name brands that dominated, and Duran Duran and Miami Vice brought us pastel suits and designer stubble, even as Tom Cruise in Top Gun made Ray Ban must-have eye wear. And let's not forget parachute pants and thin leather ties for guys and the Madonna accessories for girls. There's also the hair—the VERY BIG hair, the Jheri curl, and the bi-level, the forerunner of the mullet (which came to our town to die and never did). Of course, for most of us, we all had the same cut. But as popular as all these things were in the rest of the country, inside the hallowed halls of THS the uniform of choice (or should I say conformity?) consisted of tight, straight-leg jeans and T-shirts—with a light Member's Only jacket added during the mild North Florida winters.

As we were coming of age, so were slasher films—Michael Myers, Jason Voorhees, and Freddy Krueger were cuttin' kids like us up, and most of us couldn't get enough of it. But there were real things to be afraid of—such as Darth Vader's evil empire the Soviet Union, and the looming threat of nuclear war.

We were the first generation to get cable in our small town (the one John Mellencamp was singing so eloquently about)—and all the trauma that came with it, such as repeatedly seeing Ronald Reagan get shot. I also vividly remember a small group of us stumbling out of the art room and into the classroom next door to watch as Challenger fell from the sky, its image, along with that of school teacher Christa McAuliffe, waving as she walked toward her destiny, played over and over again until it was burned onto the screens of our minds.

In some ways, it will always be 1986 for us. Rick Springfield, Lionel Richie, Culture Club, Hall and Oates, Donna Summer (as played by the THS Marching Band, The Silver System), and Cyndi Lauper will forever be on our radios, their music the soundtrack of our lives, and in some nearby theater a Molly Ringwald movie will be playing.

Many of the things that we witnessed the birth of back in the 80s have reached maturity today (even if many of us still haven't): Digital music is no longer just on discs, but on our computers, which are no longer clunky metal masses with monochrome monitors that run on disc drives, but small, sleek machines with mega memory and a portal to the world via the connective tissue known as the Internet. The blockbuster now dominates all aspects of media and entertainment. Walmart has taken over the world, closing down some wonderful Mom and Pop shops along the way. Family farms have gone the way of pay phones. Video games (Space Invaders, Pac Man, Tron in our day) have moved out of arcades and convenience stores and into sophisticated home platforms that make what we played look like the graphic equivalent of cave drawings.

The world is changing in ways wonderful and detrimental, and we all continue to be swept along in the rolling river of life, carried by unseen currents we can neither fully understand nor control.

I can't speak for my classmates, but twenty years after the diploma was placed in my hand and my tassel was moved from one side to the other, I still feel eighteen much of the time, still feel like adults are other people— my parents and their peers, perhaps, but not me. In many ways I haven't grown up and never will. In others, I am so far from high school I can barely remember it—only the monotony, the beige, the desire to fit in and not stick out, yet the need for independence and self-expression. I remember fondly the dances following football games when we were still in junior high (slow dancing to Boz Scaggs' Look What You've Done to Me, and feeling every word of it); first love; the cool, fun teachers; and any activities that got us out of class—whether legit or not.

I haven't kept up with my former classmates very well. I have no idea what most of them are doing with their days, but I miss them like the long lost siblings they are.

One theory of the pre-life is that as souls we choose those we will join with to form a family when we reach earth. I think the same might very well be true of classmates.

Twenty years have come and gone, flying by much of the time, crawling occasionally. The world is as different a place as we are the same at our core the people we've always been. More than two decades after we sat in our last class together, we're still connected to each other, and always will be, for no more reason than that we did time together in the formative years of our lives before we were paroled for time served and good behavior, and set loose, ostensibly as adults, on the world awaiting our arrival. But that's no small bond. At least twenty of us walked into kindergarten on the first day and out of high school graduation on our last, and in the process had experiences we didn't have with any other human beings on the planet.

To my fellow classmates of the very best class ever, the Class of 1986, I love you. Thanks for all the memories—monotonous moments to milestones—and let me just say that if you're lost you can look—and you will find me—time after time. If you fall I will catch you—I'll be waiting. Time after time.

Three

It moves me, taking me back to my childhood in
a way that infuses me with the bittersweet longing for a
home that no longer exists, an experience heightened by
my absolute emotional rawness, and I'm reminded of what
Rumi said. First I was raw, then I was cooked, then I was
ash.

Thinking of Rumi reminds me of the poem that
always makes me think of Carrie.

The minute I heard my first love story
I started looking for you, not knowing
how blind that was.
Lovers don't finally meet somewhere.
They're in each other all along.

We've always been in each other. Always would be. I believed that more at this moment than ever before.

Reading what I had written for our reunion and having the Rumi lines come to mind reminds me just how random and ridiculous life can be. I'm a semi-successful writer, but my success, such as it is, comes not from what I write as much as from my translations of other writers. Writers such as Rumi. Books of my original work sell only a small fraction of my translations of the work of others. I am what I always wanted to be—a respected writer. I have a modest but growing reputation. The cruel irony is I'm known for the writing of others. For me, this sums up life perfectly. Even at its best it still retains that nearly-but-not-quite quality. Few experiences are as expected, very little works out like we want, and every edge is double-sided.

Eventually, with tears in her eyes, Carrie joins me, her soft, sweet perfume trailing behind her, drifting over me.

We sit this way for a moment, neither of us speaking, her sniffling quietly beside me, both of us facing forward, toward the coffin.

Can you believe this place? she says. Could it be any more meretricious?

I love that. Funeral parlor as whore house. It's like it all came from that catalog of cheap shit your aunt used to sell. What was—

You're right. Heart of Home Interiors. God, it was so bad. Is this what it all comes to? Does it have to be this way? End this way?

I had no answer for that—at least not one either of us would like.

Things like this always make me wonder if I'm wasting my life, I say.

Things like this?

Sudden death of someone close.

She shoots me a subtly incredulous quizzical look. You two were close?

Not as close as I'd've liked to have been. Not lately, but . . .

She nods. Did they ask you if they could display the letter?

I shake my head.

If they had?

I couldn't've said no.

She turns and looks around the empty room. Where is everybody? I thought there'd be a lot more mourners.

It's early. 'Sides, this joint does this whole funerals and visitations thing in shifts. It's Jay Bryan, Jr.'s peoples' turn right now.

Who? she asks. Oh. Another stiff?

I nod.

What if we're the only ones to show up?

That'd be just fine with me, but we won't be. There'll be lots of others.

Maybe not.

There will.

Why'd you come so early?

Honestly?

Of course.

Hoping to spend some time alone with you.

Really? Me too. I'm so glad you did.

The Rose Room is long and narrow, decorated in the same manner as the lobby and hallway. Flowers fill in the openness, placed around high-back chairs and couches along the walls, a podium with a guest book midway up, and the theater-style setup of chairs facing the coffin in the front.

Are you? she asks.

Glad I came early?

Wasting your life. You said things like this make you think you're wasting your life.

I think so—sometimes. I don't know. Not sure what else I could be doing.

Do you think we all have a vocation, a calling? A reason we were born?

I shrug. Sometimes. Others, everything seems so random.

But you knew you wanted to be a poet and a writer and all even back in school, didn't you?

I think about it for a moment. I guess. Maybe. The only thing I can say for sure is that I'm most fulfilled when I'm writing. But I wouldn't call it a calling.

I would. Why wouldn't you? That's exactly what it is and you damn well know it.

Maybe.

Absolutely.

What about you?

I was meant to act, but I never pursued it.

Why not?

Not sure exactly. It was never a good time. Things always got in the way. I kept thinking I'd get around to it one day, but just never did.

I'm sorry to hear that.

People say it's never too late, she says, but that's just not true. Sometimes it is.

I think back to her performances in our high school productions. She was transcendent as Emily in *Our Town*, angelic as Juliet in *Romeo and Juliet*, a sweet, cute, sublime Kim MacAfee in *Bye Bye Birdie*, and a sweet, sexy, sophisticated Sandy in the original raw version of *Grease* that nearly got our drama teacher fired. Was she as good as I remember? My infatuation obscures objectivity—then as now. But she was quite something as she strut her hour upon the stage. A force. I had been mesmerized. And not just me.

Descending from above, an unseen curtain of sadness closes, drifting down, darkening the memory stage in my mind, covering, stifling, suffocating, and I find her unrealized potential, her unopened gifts, her unused talents nearly as unbearable as my own.

We have such grand dreams when we're young, she says.

I nod. We did, didn't we?

You saying we're not young?

No. We are. At least . . . youngish. That's what makes this so—

Mine were nothing compared to yours. I mean, I guess I had an idea of how my life would go—and this isn't it, by the way—but I didn't have visions of grandeur.

And I did?

Didn't you? You were going to change the world.

I think about it. I was going to write profound poetry for the masses, finally pen the great American novel, make movies and music, and create a philosophy of life that was simultaneously simple and sublime.

You expect far more out of life than I do, she says. Always have.

I do?

Her attention shifts and she gazes out into the distance, seeing something not in the room, something I can't see. That kind of optimism or hope or whatever it is . . . would've killed me.

I thought about it. Hasn't worked out so well for me either, I say.

I think it has.

I let out a small, harsh laugh. Change the world. What a silly, foolish boy.

It's sweet.

Just the opposite happened.

You don't seem all that different.

It's changed me far more than I changed it.

Maybe.

Undoubtedly.

Inevitably . . . I guess.

We are quiet a moment and a muffled version of The First Noel bleeds in from the lobby.

Unbelievable, she says. I feel like a teenager. It's surreal.

I'm sure it's my fault. Don't we always revert back to

high school when we're around each other?

What, and wonder what might have been?

I nod. I know I do.

Me too.

We might have done something about what might have been if we saw each other more often than homecomings and funerals.

I think back to our various high school reunions—the awkwardness of being intimate with peers from an earlier period, now relative strangers, the inevitable comparisons, the embarrassing stories, the posturing and posing, the nursed grudges that were ridiculous to begin with, now absurd all these years later, and, for me, always the hope of seeing Carrie, of being, however briefly, with her.

As if having access to my thoughts, she says, We didn't see each other at our five-year class reunion, did we?

Were you there?

Just for a little while, she says with a frown.

I looked for you at the parade.

You weren't on the float, were you?

I shake my head. A five-year float seemed so silly to me.

Never were much of a joiner, were you?

Guess not. I tried to be cool about it, but I asked everyone I saw if they had seen you.

I did the same thing.

Her eyes narrow in concentration, then she looks up, appearing to be accessing memories. So we missed the five, she says, but we saw each other at the ten, fifteen, and twenty.

I just went hoping to see you.

Did I really just say that out loud? The surreal circumstances have me acting strange. Trying to think of something else to say. We haven't had many opportunities, have we?

To see each other? There was that one time at Christmas . . . like the song.

The song?

She sings, Met my old lover at the grocery store, snow was falling Christmas Eve.

I think of her when I hear that song, which I invariably do several times every holiday season.

Except we were merely almost lovers, I say, and it doesn't snow in Florida.

Merely?

I just meant—

I know what you meant, she says. And you're right, but it kept playing in my mind.

Really?

Still does . . . when I think back on it. And you know the strangest thing . . . In my memory of that night, it's snowing.

Are we also lovers? I ask.

She smiles a smile that manages to be both sweetly sheepish and completely wanton.

A shiver runs through me.

How much of memory is imagination? I wonder. Fantasy? Idealized, heightened reality? How much of what I remember never happened? How much of what I recall with certainty never took place?

Isn't it funny how we all have our own soundtracks? I ask.

She nods. And how they're different even when we're sharing the same moment. You tell me one.

Huh?

Since the circumstances have us being so uncharacteristically honest, share one of your songs with me.

I think about it, remembering, reliving, the song a portal to our past.

Back in school when I'd see you in the hall or at a football game or in town, I'd hear, Hello! Is it me you're looking for? I can see it in your eyes. I can see it in your smile. You're all I've ever wanted and my arms are open wide.

Me too. Me too. The exact same song. I used to drive by the groccry store when you were working and actually sing out loud, I've been alone with you inside my mind. And in my dreams I've kissed your lips a thousand times.

Sometimes our soundtracks are the same.

I bet yours and mine are a lot.

This should be embarrassing, I say, but it's not.

It's not. It's sweet.

I guess I didn't have an emotion in the 80s Lionel Richie didn't express for me.

Tell me another one.

I'll tell you two. Both by Rick Springfield. When you were dating Tony, I'd sing, I wish that I had Tony's girl. Where can I find a woman like that? Lately things have changed and it ain't hard to define. Tony's got himself a girl and I want to make her mine. And then later—our junior year, I think—I'd run through the grocery store using the broom as a guitar, singing, You better love somebody. It's gettin' late. You better love somebody. Don't wait.

You played broom guitar for me?

I did.

If I go get a broom, will you play for me now?

I smile. Maybe later.

Remember the dances?

More than I should, I'm sure.

Those are some of my fondest memories from school. The cool nights after the home football games, the dark commons, music pumping.

Mine too, I say, and instantly, as if time has folded and transported me back to those faraway falls, I am standing in the old school commons.

The tables have been removed, the chairs shoved back to the walls. One remaining table sits on the edge of the stage. It holds two turntables, two cassette decks, a mixer, and stacks of records and tapes. Behind it, one of the upperclassmen, a senior boy with a band, serves as DJ, spinning the tunes he knows will keep everybody on the floor.

From across the room, through the twisting couples, I see her, standing alone, waiting. I'm waiting too—for the perfect slow song to come on. I've got a few in mind— Sailing, Truly, and—and then the one I want most of all comes on. Boz Scaggs' Look What You've Done To Me.

I reach her before the intro is over.

Wanna dance?

Unsuccessfully suppressing a smile, she nods. I'd love to.

I take her hand and lead her to the dance floor, where earlier today we sat at tables forking through uneatable food.

Hope they never end this song.
This could take us all night long.

This may be the final song of the evening, and it couldn't be more fitting. It captures how I feel, what I want to say, how I want things to be.

I hold her so close, I fear one of the chaperones might come break us up at any moment. Few things would be more embarrassing, but I can't stop, can't pull back.

The sweet floral smell of her hair is intoxicating, her skin hot, her hand moist like mine.

Take me up your stairs and through the door.
Take me where we don't care anymore.

She asks, What was the Lionel Richie song we used to dance to?

Back in the present as instantly as I had been in the past, as if they're occurring simultaneously, as if she and I will always be dancing in the Tupelo High School commons, I clear my throat and say, We danced to all of them. Think maybe we still are.

Really? That's romantic as fuck. I love it. But we danced to this one more than all the others. Slow song. It was so sweet, so tender. A duet.

With Diana Ross. Endless Love.

Yeah, that's it. It was so . . .

I know. You smelled so good, your skin and breath so warm. And your hair. I'd rest my head on yours and just breathe in the scent of your hair. Here, let me show you.

I stand, take her hand, help her up, and we begin to slow dance as I softly sing in her ear.

My love. There's only you in my life. The only thing that's right.

She responds, My first love, you're every breath I take. You're every step I make.

We could press our bodies against each other so tight, she adds.

Like this? I say, pulling her even closer. I loved the way your breasts felt against my chest. Still do.

I could tell, she says, and swallows hard. God, feeling your . . . ah, response, just sent me. Still does.

I actually felt drunk.

I wish we could go back there right now.

Me too.

I'd figure out some way to make sure we wound up together.

I stop, her words a harsh reminder that we didn't, that she's not mine, that we're not back in school slow dancing after a football game.

Awkwardly, we make our way back to our seats.

The door in the back opens and a young man in a cheap black suit brings in more flowers, finds a place for them, then leaves, closing the door behind him. I'm grateful he didn't come in a few moments earlier.

I know this is going to make me sound old, but our music was so much more romantic, she says. Today it's all hittin' dat shorty, tappin' dat ass, and gettin' paid.

You're right, I say. That does make you sound old.

She punches me in the arm, her small fist frogging my muscle the way it did so long ago.

But you're right about the music, I say.

Who do you think sees the world more clearly? Us or them?

You mean as teenagers? I ask.

Yeah. Romance or cynicism?

Is that a trick question? No one sees the world clearly. Especially teenagers.

You know what I mean.

I prefer ours, but, of course, I would, wouldn't I?

You sound British.

Does one? Bloody sorry, old chap. How about, Dude, ours rocks, theirs sucks?

Much better.

We fall silent a moment.

Time passes. And some more. And then some more. It always is. Never stops. Never relents, never, not even for one merciful moment.

I wrote a story about us—about how I wish it would've been. I have it with me if you want to read it.

Can I?

Would you?

Why do you have it with you?

Can I tell you later?

Of course.

I hand her the folded sheets of printer paper, and, opening them, she leaves me here and now in this world to join another me in another world, which is all that makes her departure bearable.

It's called Seventeen, I say.

Four

Seventeen

You are seventeen.

She is sixteen.

You were made for each other. How two halves of the same soul had journeyed so far, wound up in the same small town, and found each other is truly astonishing, but because you are so young, because this is so new—you are both so new on this old planet in this ancient universe—you don't realize just how astonishing it really is.

You even look like each other—so much so that when your brandy-brown eyes meet, the amber pools you're diving into are reflections of the depths she too is plumbing.

People call what you feel for her infatuation, but you

call it love. Except, not even love is a strong enough word for what you feel for this girl. The girl. The only girl in the world.

What you feel for her, what she feels for you—for it is the same emotion, the same experience—is ageless, eternal, like your essence loved her essence in whatever place they were in before they came to this place. The way you love her here and now in this world is so total, so all consuming, that it couldn't have just started, but must have begun back before humans, before the universe, before time. No wonder people say God is love. For you, now, though, love is God. You look at her and you finally understand what God meant, what she was trying to communicate with her pen and palette.

You meet in high school.

You love her the moment you see her. Love everything about her. Not just her beauty—what was it Keats said? Beauty is truth. The truth of her beauty is obvious, apparent to everyone. But you, you love her very soul—what was the other thing Keats said? Truth is beauty—that numinous quality beneath the beauty that animates and attracts. You love her blood, her breath, the wrinkled bottoms of her feet, every seen and unseen thing about her.

Of beauty being truth and truth beauty, Keats said, that is all ye know on earth, and all ye need to know. But, you think, she is all I know on earth. She is all I need to know.

She is quiet. Shy. If not for how pretty she is, she would be overlooked completely. As it is, others think she is attractive, but miss how alluring her more subtle attributes are. But you don't. You see her. Really see all that she is. And not just. You see more. For in the girl she is, you see the woman she'll become.

In the small rises beneath her cotton candy-pink nipples, you see the full, nourishing, life-giving breasts she'll one day have. In the narrow fingers laced between yours, you see the strong, elegant hands that will one day do such great things—reaching out, lifting up, creating, loving, pointing, gripping (you if you're lucky, as she takes you in her hand and leads you to her soft, wet, wanting mouth). You see past her too-thin appendages and slight frame, to the full, curvaceous female she will one day be.

She steps out of the cruel conformity and mind-numbing monotony of the prison called high school, and she makes it not just bearable, but pleasurable. You'll gladly endure fifty minutes of any subject, no matter how irrelevant, taught by any teacher, no matter how tedious, just for the five minutes with her it buys you between the classes.

You don't know it, how could you? But what you have for her, with her, what you receive from her, is so pure, so untainted and uncomplicated that you'll never experience it again. Only when you're older, only when you witness the wanting way most people relate and call it love will you truly know how rare and flawless and simple and profound what you had was—but, of course, then it'll be too late. Youth is wasted on the young, your grandfather used to say, and now you know. When you are older, you will be heard to say, Young love is wasted on young lovers.

Not that you wasted your love for her. You didn't.

Every cell loves her. Every single cell. You hold nothing back, keep nothing in reserve. As a newborn, as a child, as a teenager, you have been thoroughly and completely loved. Your father is kind and generous, your mother encouraging and nurturing. You've received so much love, you have so much love, and you lavish it all on her. You love her to extreme, to excess.

You find her mind amazing, a potent aphrodisiac. She is clever, a genuine wit, her intelligence and insight manifesting in her humor, her hilarious observations. She is cerebral and it's sexy. She is highly intellectual and you find it highly erotic.

You can't even imagine your life without her in it. All talk of the future involves planning to be together. Marriage is fine. It doesn't matter what you call it. What you have with her transcends ceremonies, legalities, institutions. It's from before such things existed. It'll be around long after such things are extinct.

You've never before found someone as open and unguarded as you are. You talk like the truest of friends, share everything—every fear, every dream, every minute detail of every day. You stay on the phone into the early morning hours, your warm ear moist with sweat, your fingers stiff from gripping the receiver, your throat dry, voice sleepy, lids too heavy to stay open.

You love everything about her, especially the indescribable, ineffable essence of her—what? Soul? Your expression of that all-encompassing love is verbal, is word and deed, but mostly it is corporal. You worship her body, sure, but it's more than that. Your love for every aspect of her, of her very quiddity is expressed, is focused, is lavished in extravagance on her body.

You love her mind, but you can't kiss her mind, so you kiss her mouth—long, slow explorations of her warm, wet mouth. The taste of her, like the smell of her, sends you like nothing else.

You love her heart, but you can't touch her heart, so you touch her chest, the smooth valley between her small, firm, beautiful breasts.

Her breasts.

The shape of her breasts, the way they're perched upon the plate of her chest, the way they hang above her torso, like sweet fruit at the peak of its ripeness. Fruit you savor and devour and enjoy and yet is still there to be savored and devoured and enjoyed every time you come back wanting to this tree of life.

Back to kissing.

You love to kiss her. You do it for hours at a time. And not just her lips, her mouth, but all of her—especially her fingertips and toes.

You like the smell of her hair when you kiss her neck, and the way it mingles with the hint of her perfume.

You love it that she wears no makeup, that everywhere your lips touch, your tongue tastes, is just her—unvarnished, unaltered, undeniably her. Skin to skin. Flesh to flesh.

You love the way she gives herself to you. She holds nothing back. She trusts you. She knows you love her, knows you'll take care of her, protect her, guard her dignity, keep her secrets, and this frees her, makes her want to make of herself the gift you most want to receive.

You've yet to make love to her, to put your love inside of hers and create even more. It's something you don't take lightly. You realize what it means, what it will cost—both of you, but her more than you.

You talk often of running away together. You have nothing to run away from. You both have good lives, good homes, good parents. It's not what you're running away from, but what you'd be running away to—to be together. To be alone. To be on your own. It's a romantic notion, pure fantasy, and you both know it, but it doesn't stop you from dreaming, from wishing, from wanting it in the way that only wanting something you can't have can make you want something.

Every time you're alone—every single time—you talk about leaving the small town behind and starting your future lives together now, but you talk about it most in the afternoons, that magical time between school and your parents coming home from work. If you ever do run away, at least run far enough to elope, to return secretly as husband and wife to your high school life, this is the time—these afternoon hours—that you'll do it. So that's the time you talk about it.

Run away with me, you say.

Okay, she says.

I mean right now.

Me too.

You'll really run away with me right now?

Now. Later. Tomorrow. Next Tuesday. Whenever

you want.

She tells you she's yours and that she wants to take your name. You tell her you're hers and you want to take her name.

When people see you together, overhear the things you say, chance upon a note of affection, they shake their heads, embarrassed—and not just for themselves, but for you. How silly, they say. What fools you are. Grow up. Get real. You think you're in love, but you're not. It's just hormones, just chemicals playing tricks on you.

You feel sorry for them, feel pity that they don't have what you have. If they did, or ever had, they'd get it, but they haven't, so they don't. They're missing out on the best part of life, the part that makes all the others parts better, or at least bearable.

When they tell you that you'll grow out of it, you realize that what they're saying is that somewhere along the way, they have lost their way, have lost love. It reminds you of the seven-year-old boy who crept to his newborn brother's crib in the middle of the night and said, Tell me about God. I'm starting to forget.

What you have for this girl isn't something you grow out of, can't be reduced to adolescent chemicals or inexperience with emotions. It's original, essential, elemental, everlasting.

Your junior prom falls on her seventeenth birthday, and you decide that's the day to accept the gift she keeps trying to give you.

The gift you will give her, the one so few girls ever get, is a tender, romantic, fantastic first time.

Beneath a full moon, you drive to the beach in your father's big old Ford, the backseat littered with bathing suits, towels, a change of clothes, and the crown and tiara the two of you were given when, earlier in the magical night, you became prom king and queen. She sits next to you, her dress filling up the front seat, her head on your shoulder. The windows are down and the smell of her hair and perfume waft over in the wind.

You find a secluded spot in the sand, far away from the bonfires and drunken silliness of classmates here for reasons that seem similar, but couldn't be more different.

The Gulf is calm, its smooth, gently undulating surface reflecting the pale face of the nocturnal orb, as if a rare gem seen in dark glass.

Sea oats sway rhythmically in the evening breeze, their dance not unlike the rolling waters or the sacred movements you two will soon be making.

Between rising dunes, you spread out a sheet that smells as fresh as a summer field after an afternoon shower, and lie down in your roofless bedroom beneath the shimmering, winking stars.

The sand is cool and lumpy beneath the sheet, and you both wiggle your bodies to smooth out your ageless bed, dream dust of God, like two coquina boring into the shore following the returning of the tide.

For a long moment, you lie beside each other looking up at infinity, then turning toward one another, you look into eternity.

Slowly, carefully, you undress her, kissing her back as you unzip her dress. Her skin is tan and smooth and warm.

When she is nude, her dress and undergarments placed carefully aside, you, still fully clothed, stare down at her moonlit nubility, and beneath your beating heart, your breath catches.

No one has ever felt this way before, you think, even as you realize the feeling is as old as any feeling in existence.

Neither afraid nor ashamed, she looks up at you, a sweet sensuousness in her face, a dance of light in her eyes.

Lying back as she is, her small breasts are completely flat, only her pink nipples protruding above the surface of her chest.

You watch her watch you as you undress, carefully extending your briefs over your full, erect phallus—at which her eyes widen and her mouth opens into a small O.

Lying atop her, but not yet entering her, you kiss her—first her mouth, then her neck, then her ears, whispering how beautiful she is and how much you love her as you do. You then work your way down her body, unintentionally tickling her as you skip across her rib cage and down her sides.

She stops laughing when you move to her nipples, her breath catching, her pulse increasing even more, and the sweetest little sounds coming involuntarily from her mouth.

From her breasts, you move toward her most sacred, intimate place, lingering on her flat tummy, the tip of your tongue darting into her small navel as you do.

And then you move lower.

And then you're home.

You've never felt such soft, wet warmth in all your

life. This is what love feels like, you think. What God tastes like.

You don't want to stop. You want to keep kissing her here all night, but she is ready—waiting and wanting.

You rise up, holding yourself above her, and in her desire, in her impatience, she takes you in her hand and guides you back into Eden, to the garden of pure delight.

You okay? you ask her.

Never better in my entire life. Will never be any better than this moment—even if I live to be . . . forever. This is it, you think. What you've been missing, longing for. This is heaven. This is the meaning of life.

After a while, when you can no longer wait, when you reach the point at which you could sooner hold back the tide, you hear a sound in your ears, and you're not sure if it's the love-rich blood racing through your veins, or the wind and the waves, or the flap and flutter of angels. You just know you've never heard anything more beautiful—or ever will.

Happy seventeenth birthday, baby, you say, when you're able to speak again.

Yes, she says. It is.

Five

It's so beautiful, she whispers.

She folds the pages, presses them to her face as if to smell or kiss them, then handing them back to me with tears in her eyes, she says, That is us. Was us. That really happened.

What?

In some reality, some dimension, some version of ourselves really experienced that. I believe it. I know it.

Then I do too.

And now this version of ourselves has too. It's so beautiful.

Thank you.

You did it. You became what you set out to be.

You're so good.

I shake my head, tears stinging my eyes. There's nothing to it. It's just a simple little story no one will ever see.

I saw it.

Yes, you did. And that's all that matters. Truly. It's all I ever wanted. You to read it, experience it.

And it's not simple or little. It's beautiful, it's . . . like so very many times before, words you wrote move me, touch me, heal me, change me. That's you changing the world—just like you said you were going to.

Wouldn't it be pretty to think so?

She doesn't respond, and we fall quiet again.

Eventually, inevitably, we both wind up staring at the coffin.

Can you believe we're here for this?

Actually, I can't, and I'm trying not to think about it.

The thing about life is that we die, she says. Wonder why? Why do we die? Why do we have to? Seems like such sad and ridiculous waste.

It is. It totally is. Just about the time we figure a few things out, we buy it.

And life goes on, she adds. We'll be gone and life just goes on for everybody else.

I resent the fuck out of that, I say.

I know. Me too. It's not a party if we're not here. I want to live so bad. You know I've never had a single suicidal thought.

Me either.

Can you imagine cutting this shorter than it already

is? Even by one moment? One breath? Most of us would give anything for more time, even for a just a little, and others willingly, violently, carelessly cash out with decades left.

Has to be mental illness. Nothing else makes sense. Plenty of people have unimaginably difficult lives and they don't do it.

Don't you wish they could give it to you?

What?

At work, when someone is really sick and has burned through all their leave time, we can donate some of ours to them. I wish those who don't want all their life time could give it to those who want all ours and more.

I nod, thinking what a great concept, but also knowing what inspired it.

When I was going through my treatment, she says, my coworkers, my friends were so generous with their sick leave. They gave me weeks' and weeks' worth.

I feel guilty and ashamed and had wanted to avoid the subject of her sickness.

I didn't know you went through that until just recently, I say. I'm so sorry. Wish I had known. Wish I could've been there for you. Wish I had had sick leave to donate to you.

Let's not talk about that, she says. That's all over now and I don't like even thinking about it.

I'm sorry.

What sorry? she says. I brought it up.

Sorry I wasn't there for you. Sorry you had to go through all that without me.

She nods. That's what I meant. I fought so hard to live, to get better, and some people are perfectly healthy and throw it all away.

I know.

As I close my eyes to try to stop my tears, my lids press them out of the corners and onto my beginning-to-crinkle skin, and I wipe at them.

Do you feel old? she asks.

I shake my head. Not at all, I say. I feel so good. Sitting here with you . . . I feel . . . I'm not sure they've come up with a word for it. You?

Me?

Feel old?

No. Not most of the time. Most of the time I still feel like the girl in your story. But so much time has passed. So much has happened.

Yet our junior high dances seem like yesterday.

It was twenty-five years ago, she says.

Not possible. I don't even really feel like a grownup. An adult, maybe, but not a grownup.

You're older now than your parents were then.

No, I say. I can't—I really am. Wonder if they felt the same way.

Wonder if they still do?

You think at sixty-five they still feel like they're twenty-something?

We don't feel much different than we did twenty years ago. Will we feel so different twenty years from now?

Why didn't anyone tell us?

She laughs. Are you telling anyone?

Such as?

I don't know. Random teenagers you meet. Young adults you encounter.

I'm a young adult.

No you're not. Young adults don't know who Lionel Richie is. They know Nicole, but not Lionel.

Who?

She laughs and shakes her head.

I'm not a young adult anymore, am I?

Sorry, she says, biting her lip. And you've got people close to you dying.

Not of old age.

Age was a factor.

How you figure?

The longer you live, the greater your chance of buying it.

I guess.

She stands, looking around. I can't believe more people aren't here.

They will be. Soon. Too soon.

What?

I just wish we could stay like this.

It is nice.

I take her hand and pull her back down beside me. She sits, still looking around, distracted. I don't let go.

Who would've thought we'd get another chance? she asks.

After blowing so many?

I just meant . . . and under these circumstances . . . I never would've believed it.

How honest we gonna be here? I ask. The situation has me feeling like I'm in a confessional.

Ever been in a confessional?

No. You?

Not really. No.

Well, either you have or you haven't.

She laughs. Not to confess or anything, but I did look inside one once while in Italy.

I didn't know you went to Italy.

I take a trip every summer.

I never knew.

Why would you?

I wouldn't, I say, frowning. I'd just want to.

She's lived a lifetime I'll never know about, I think. Gone places, done things, met people, had experiences—all without me. A pang of longing shoots through me, and I'm suddenly jealous of all the nameless people and places who got more of her than I did over the years. Unbidden, the familiar sonnet wanders into my mind.

> Being your slave, what should I do but tend
> Upon the hours and times of your desire?
> I have no precious time at all to spend, Nor services
> to do, till you require.
> Nor dare I question with my jealous thought
> Where you may be, or your affairs suppose,
> But, like a sad slave, stay and think of nought
> Save, where you are how happy you make those.
> So true a fool is love that in your will,
> Though you do anything, he thinks no ill.

She was mine first. I should have been with her in Italy. It should have been me she was confessing her true love's vow to in the confessional of the ancient cathedral.

Still looking off, I say, We've been out of each other's lives longer than we were in them.

Missed so much, she says.

Too much.

We drift into heavy, oppressive silence.

She says, I'll be as honest as you will.

Huh?

You asked how honest we're going to be.

Okay, I say. I've always carried a torch for you. It's never died out. It almost has a few times, but then I'd see you at a class reunion or a funeral and it'd get rekindled.

That's your big revelation?

Pretty much, yeah.

Kind of obvious, isn't it? I thought everybody knew.

I laugh. Really?

I think how we feel about each other is obvious to everyone.

You feel the same way?

Of course, you idiot.

Still?

Yes.

Well, I've never come out and just said it quite like that.

You didn't have to, she says.

Well, this time I felt like I should.

I'm glad you did. I'm just saying I already knew.

I'm that obvious?

The way you look at me.

How's that?

Like I'm the meaning of life.

I smile. I guess I do, don't I?

But I'm not, am I?

Can't say for sure.

Sure you can. Rarely do we not know the truth. We might not like it, might not want to admit it—even to ourselves, but we usually know it.

I've yet to find the meaning of life, so I can't say that you aren't it.

You really haven't? Better hurry, she adds, nodding toward the coffin.

I know, right?

I thought there would be more people. I'm really surprised.

There will be.

I just feel bad for the poor stiff.

Well, don't. There'll be a good turnout.

I don't know.

I look at my watch. It's early still. Come on, let's get out of here.

We can't.

I stand and pull her up.

Just for a few minutes. This little room is closing in on us.

I don't know. What if—

Come on.

Shaking her head and scrunching her face, she slowly

begins to follow me. Reaching the door, I open it and wait, allowing her to go first, but she stops.

What is it?

I . . . I'm just not sure.

I am.

Six

Stepping through the open door, I pull her hand. She hesitates, but then stops resisting and joins me in the ornately decorated hallway.

Rather than returning the way I came in earlier, I turn to the left, leading her through the back hallway and into the family lounge.

Family lounge? Carrie says, looking around. Fancy name for a few tables, two vending machines, and a coffee pot.

I laugh.

The lounge is small and unimpressive, a typical corporate break room—with the addition of some children's toys and books in one corner.

What else they gonna call it? I ask.

How about break room? Or . . . Why does it have to have a name?

It's better than the Rose Room.

She laughs.

You want some coffee or something?

She shakes her head. I'm good.

I pull out a chair for her, and we sit at one of the small tables.

Yes, she says, a wry expression transforming her face from beautiful to cute, this is much better.

It may not be better, but it's different.

You like different, don't you?

You don't?

Not as much.

I can tell she has more to say.

Let's have it.

Huh?

What's wrong with liking different?

Nothing . . . as long as it's not just restlessness.

I start to say something, but stop, and think about my lonesome, never-satisfied nature. Am I just restless or is it because I haven't been with her? Is she the home I've been longing for?

She says, What you're looking for isn't out there, it's in here.

Seriously? The family lounge?

I mean it, she continues, the meaning of life, the fulfillment that seems so elusive, it's within you. Everything you need, you already have.

Almost everything.

A small boy of about seven in a tiny black suit and tie opens the door and walks in, his little fingers grasping a couple of quarters. Making his way over to the drink machine, he pushes up on his tiptoes and feeds the coins into the slot. Pressing the button, he steps back and waits.

Nothing happens.

I hop up and step over to him. I think you need one more quarter, buddy. Let's see what I've got.

Rummaging around the keys and mints in my pocket, I finally come out with a shiny new quarter and thumb it into the slot.

Now try it.

The little fellow does. And this time a series of mechanical noises results in a can drink dropping into the opening in front of him.

Thank you, he says, his voice soft.

Popping the top immediately, he begins to slurp down the sugary soda as he slowly walks out of the room.

You're a good dad, aren't you? Carrie says as I rejoin her at the table.

Honestly? I rock. It's one of the few things at which I genuinely excel.

I knew it. Not the few things excelling part. I know better than that. But I knew you'd make a great dad. Knew it even back in school.

It's a priority, you know? I work at it—a lot, but the

truth is I have a lot to work with. Jason is . . . he's just the best.

Two little girls in dark dresses and black patent shoes enter the room, their small hands grasping dollar bills.

I stand and reach for Carrie's hand. Come on.

Where're we going?

My car.

We should probably go back in.

We've spent our lives doing what we should probably do.

So why stop now?

I can think of at least one good reason.

She nods and gives me an I guess expression—raised eyebrows, twisted-lip frown raising into a smile.

Seven

Forget about the meaning of life for a moment, she says, and just tell me some of the things in your life you find meaningful.

I finally have her in my car after all these years and instead of making out, she's talking about the meaning of life.

The vehicle, my dream car, is a new Shelby Mustang, black with gray racing stripes, a scoop, and hood pins.

This car is supposed to make women take their panties off right away, I say.

She laughs. Did it actually say that on the sticker?

I nod. Why I bought it.

Has it worked?

On every girl but you.

Let's finish our current conversation, then we'll see what happens.

This is our current conversation.

She shakes her head. Meaning . . .

I'd find it particularly meaningful if you'd take off your panties.

Be serious, she says.

I am.

What else?

You.

She smiles.

I mean it. You've always given me . . . hope. Love.

Okay. What else?

Jason.

She nods.

My writing. Creating. Being creative. Writing my own stuff instead of translating others.

Are you making enough time in your life to do that?

Not enough. Not lately. I'm sorry, Mom. I'll do better.

Am I mothering you? I don't mean to. I just worry about you.

I know, I say. I'm sure I could do with some more. Mothering?

Well, yeah. But I meant time for more creativity.

Well, what're you waiting for? The death of someone close?

Yes, I think that might just do it. Unless I find that

I'm just too depressed to create now.

What creative act gives you the most meaning?

You know the answer.

Say it again. Out loud.

Writing poetry.

And how much of your life are you spending doing it?

Not nearly enough. Bills and all.

Do you find meaning in paying your bills?

Yes, that was going to be next on my list.

What else?

Talking with you. Like this. Now take off your clothes.

The search for meaning is itself meaningful. Just the belief that there is meaning is meaningful. You know?

I will if you take off your clothes. I really will. I'll believe in meaning, in God, in goodness, in love, in us.

I've always believed in us. Always.

Help me believe too. Take off your panties.

We better get back inside, she says, opening the door.

I reach past her and pull the door closed and lock it.

What're you—

I'm not going to let us keep making the same mistakes over and over again.

But . . .

But what?

We're in a car.

Yeah?

In a public parking lot.

Yeah?

At a funeral.

You're going to have to come up with something better than that. What if this is it? Our last shot? If my funeral is next, I wouldn't want to not have done this. Come on. If you don't fuck at a funeral, then where? You're the very one who said—

I know what I said.

I'm not taking no for an answer. I know you want this as much as I do.

She shakes her head.

What?

More, she says. I want it more.

I crank the car and back it into the far corner of the lot, beneath the low-hanging limbs of an overgrown oak and in between a cinderblock building that most likely houses the crematorium and a black funeral home van. From the backseat I withdraw a corrugated cardboard window shade that has the Mustang emblem on it—silver pony racing across red, white, and blue bars—stretch it across the front windshield, and flip down the sun visors to hold it into place. We have as much privacy as we're going to get.

Leaving the car idling and the heat on, I reach over her, pull up the lever, and recline her seat, then bring up the 80s love song playlist I created for this exact eventuality.

Hope they never end this song
This could take us all night long
I looked at the moon and I felt blue
Then I looked again and I saw you

This couldn't be more perfect if I scripted it, I think.

Thank you, she says.

For?

Not taking no for an answer.

Thank you for letting me not.

Taking her face in my hands, I kiss her—gently at first, but soon passionately, deeply, forcefully.

Her mouth tastes of spearmint and my tongue cannot get enough of hers.

Releasing her face, I continue to kiss her as my hands explore her body, unbuttoning, unzipping, seeking access, searching for entry.

Her skin is soft and smooth and cool to the touch.

The car should warm up in a few minutes.

I'm not cold. I'm . . . I've never been happier. Is it bad that a funeral is the best day of my life?

Sorry we're in a car.

You kidding? This isn't just a car. It's a work of art. And it's not just any car, it's yours. And our first time should be in a car. Could anything be more high school?

Only in dreams could it be this way
When you love someone, yeah, really love someone
Now I know it's right, from the moment I wake up
till deep in the night
There's nowhere on earth that I'd rather be than
holding you tenderly

As I return to kissing her neck, I unhook her bra

and finally gain access to the breasts I've longed for and dreamed about for over two decades. Her breasts are soft and substantial, their heft in my hands making me harder than I have ever been. Her nipples are huge and erect, and as I take them in my fingers she moans softly in my ear.

God, I've wanted this, waited for this, so long.

Unable to wait any longer, I lift her dress over her head. As I do, she shrugs out of her dangling bra and shimmies out of her stockings and panties.

And then she is completely naked on the leather seat of my Shelby and I am speechless.

Watching every motion in my foolish lover's game
On this endless ocean finally lovers know no shame
Turning and returning to some secret place inside
Watching in slow motion as you turn around and say

Her breasts rest on her ribcage as if perched there by a skilled sculptor. Her pale skin is flawless, accentuating the dark hair framing her face, draping her shoulders, vining the V between her legs.

My eyes have never drunk in so much beauty in all their thirsty years.

You are far more beautiful than I ever imagined.

You like?

I've never liked anything more.

You should've seen the twenty-year-old version.

Couldn't be any better than this. You are perfect, I say, and lean in and begin to kiss her taut little tummy.

As I work my way down to the mound of dark hair

between her legs, I lift up and say, I'm so so so so glad you don't shave.

Really?

Truly, I say, and bury my face in her sweet garden. She smells so good. Breathing her in, I take great sensual pleasure in every deep inhalation. Her hair feels so good on my face only one thing could make me move.

As I move my mouth below her mound and glide the tip of my tongue across her sex, she grabs my head hard with both her hands and begins to breathe and moan loudly. She tastes so good. Her wet warmth feels so good in my mouth and on my tongue.

For a surreal moment it is as if I am floating above us, looking down, unable to quite believe I am kissing Carrie Ann Winslow so intimately, so deeply.

I have wanted to be this way with her since the moment we met, and for so many years now I have wanted nothing more. Is this really happening? Does life sometimes, just sometimes, give us what we want?

I am brought back from observer to actor by her increased arousal and intensity with which she moans and grips my head. Her voice is so sweet, so soft and little-girl-like in her altered ecstatic state. She has relinquished all control and her precious panting and sweet erotic sounds are nearly more than I can take. I have never heard her quite like this, and it sends me in ways nothing in my life ever has.

And as she pulls me into her even harder and comes in my mouth, she says my name in a breathless, beautiful way that makes that which is so familiar to me something wholly new and entirely holy, and I want to hear that utterance on that tongue for the rest of my life.

Oh my God, she says. That was . . . you are . . . that was the most intense orgasm of my life—by far. I want you in me. Can we do that?

I kick off my shoes, snatch off my socks, pull down my pants, peel my underwear over my erection, and climb over the console into the reclined seat, settling on top of her.

Oh my.

With my coat, shirt, and tie still on, I slide inside her, my hardness slipping into her soft wetness with poetic perfection.

> Do I stand in your way, or am I the best thing you've had?
> Believe me, believe me, I can't tell you why
> But I'm trapped by your love, and I'm chained to your side
> We are young, heartache to heartache we stand
> No promises, no demands

Feet pressed hard against the floorboard below the dash, I fuck her hard, the leather seat below us moist with our lovemaking.

Oh God, she says.

I kiss her deep and long.

I can taste myself on your tongue, she says, in your mouth. It's so good. We're so . . .

I cup her breast with one hand and cover her mouth

with the other and fuck her even harder.

Oh God, she says into my hand. It's muffled but I can make it out. Oh fuck. Oh baby. You feel so . . . no one has ever filled me up so . . . Oh God. You're gonna make me . . . I'm gonna come again.

With that she does and, unable to hold back one moment longer, I do too.

Later, lying on her, my head on her breasts, I say, I love you. I have always loved you.

I have always loved you, E.

Eight

Returning to the empty room still straightening our clothes, she says, I can't believe there's still no one here.

You say it like it's a bad thing. I was praying there wouldn't be.

Why?

You know why. So we can stay like this for a little longer.

Let's see who sent flowers.

She moves from arrangement to arrangement, from wreath to wreath, inspecting the cards, trying to place the names, make connections.

I follow her, knowing the others will be here soon. There's very little time left. Whatever I want to say to her, I must say now.

The way I feel reminds me of the time when, returning from the storage closet in the art room after cleaning up following a junior high dance, we found ourselves locked in the school. Just the two of us. All alone. I wanted to kiss her, to tell her how I felt, but instead I worked on breaking us out. I'm not going to make the same mistake now, not going to put off any longer what's already decades overdue.

I take in a breath, let it out, and say, Why didn't we end up together? I thought we would, you know. Even after all this time, I thought one day . . . we'd have our marriages and raise our kids, but one day we'd be each other's.

She stops peering down at the card in the potted plant, straightens up and says, Somewhere in a hidden place in my heart I thought the same thing. So, why didn't we?

One of those mysteries of life, I say. You make what seems like a small decision, choose a path, take a turn—none of it seeming to amount to much, but because of the way, way leads to way, you wind up pushing forty in close proximity to a friend who is about to be pushing daises and you think, where did all the time go?

I love that you said that.

What?

Way leads to way. I was just thinking of that poem. Whose class did we learn that in?

Eleventh grade English Lit. Mrs. Wallace.

Do you remember the whole thing?

I'm not sure, I say, then pause a moment to think about it. Two roads diverged in a yellow wood . . . And sorry I could not travel both . . . And be one traveler, long I stood . . . And looked down one as far as I could . . . To where it bent in the undergrowth.

Then took the other, as just as fair, she says. And having perhaps the better claim . . . Because it was grassy and wanted wear . . . Though as for that the passing there, Had worn them really about the same.

The other way wasn't just as fair, I say. Not even close. Nor the better claim.

And in any case, I had the prior claim. You were mine first. Do you remember the next stanza?

I may need some help with it.

I'll get you started. And both that morning equally lay, In leaves . . .

No step had trodden black. Oh, I kept the first for another day!—That's what I did. I kept you for another day.

That's why I've been thinking about it too. Yet knowing how way leads on to way, I doubted if I should ever come back.

Yet knowing how way leads on to way, I repeat, tears stinging my eyes. I really didn't know.

I know. I shall be telling this with a sigh, Somewhere ages and ages hence: Two roads diverged in a wood, and I—I took the one less traveled by, And that has made all the difference.

Who wrote that? Frost, right?

Ages and ages hence. It doesn't seem like twenty years ago that we graduated. I thought we'd finally get together at our ten-year reunion.

Me too.

Do you remember what you told me?

I'm sure I told you a lot—most of it not worth remembering or repeating.

You said . . . You said, If it's true that the cells of a normal human body are completely replaced every seven years, then we have all new bodies since the last time we saw each other.

And you said, I don't feel new. I feel young—especially when I'm with you—but not all new.

I remember that like it was last night. And that night seemed like we had just graduated the night before. But in both cases a decade had passed.

God, I was so miserable in my marriage.

I could tell. But you didn't say anything, didn't try anything with me, and of course you wouldn't, would you? You never cheated on Julie, did you?

I've been alone with you inside my mind. And in my dreams I've kissed your lips a thousand times.

To use another song from our era, affairs of the heart don't count.

Ours does. It counts . . . for everything.

She doesn't respond, and we are quiet for a moment.

I like that about you.

What? My comfortable silences?

The way you were with Julie—the way you remained faithful when you were so unhappy. The sort of man you are.

I wish I'd've been a different sort of man.

No you don't. I don't.

I do. I've wasted so much time. I wish then I'd've

been like I am now. Wish I'd known then what I know now—that it didn't have to be an either-or, all-or-nothing decision.

It's what we're taught. Whatta you gonna do? Besides, it was right then. Just like where you are now is right for you now. It's a journey. We can't skip ahead.

Guess not.

Can't skip ahead, but I was hoping we could go back.

Go back? How?

You know, the universe stops expanding, reaches the end of its gravitational tether and snaps back, shrinking in on itself. Time running backward, broken teacups reassembling, spilled milk unspilling, uncouples coupling. I've always liked that idea, time and space collapsing so we would get a second chance. I would run backwards right into your arms. And never leave. And even if it all collapsed into a singularity out of which another big bang gave birth to another universe, I'd be with you. In that universe we'd be together.

Goddamn but I love the way you think, I say.

She smiles her sweet little-girl-like smile and we grow quiet a moment.

Why'd you stay? she asks.

In my marriage? I ask. For my son. He's the reason we got married in the first place. God, we were so young. And so different.

He the only reason you stayed?

I shake my head. Marriage is such a mystery. My parents' was to me, but my own is even more so. Julie was happy. Jason was happy. How could I . . . And . . . I couldn't imagine being only a part-time dad.

You're such a—

The ironic thing is we're getting divorced.

You are?

My goal was to wait 'til Jason went off to college, but we didn't quite make it. He's a junior—in the same high school we went to. He's truly been my best friend for so long . . . Now things are different. He blames me for the divorce. Sees the pain his mom is in and . . . They're not terrible, just different. We're not as close and it's killing me. I miss him so much, miss the way we . . .

As I start to cry, she pulls me into her and holds me. I'm so sorry, she says. It'll get better. You guys will be even closer.

I don't know.

I do. He's got the best dad in the world. Of course you'll always be his best friend too.

We are quiet a long moment, her comforting and holding me, and all the while time unflappably flowing forward.

And you and marriage? I say.

I've never given my heart to anyone the way I gave it to you. And I've always held some in reserve for you. Eventually, no matter how thick they are, boyfriends and husbands pick up on that. In my marriage I was more of a mom than a wife, we were more co-parents than a couple. And for a while there—and not a little while, I'm ashamed to say—I lost myself, became . . . I became just a full-time mom and part-time wife . . . and then I was nothing, a non-being. Didn't exist.

I shook my head, my heart hurting for her.

It was bad enough I was a ghost in your life, but to be a ghost in my own . . .

I'm so sorry.

It's not uncommon at all for . . . well, for women of a certain age. And maybe it's been that way for most women of every age.

I wish I had known, wish I could've done something, tried something to help in some way.

It's just life and there's nothing you can do about that.

But you can. You can help each other and make life better.

You can't know how many times I started to call you, tried to tell you, but . . . I just couldn't, couldn't do that to . . . well, any of us.

Fuck, I say shaking my head. You have any idea how often I've dreamt of you over the years? Woken up craving you, so turned-on I couldn't go back to sleep. How many times I've said your name in my sleep and had my wife ask me what I said, who I meant? How often I thought I'd die if I didn't see you?

She touches my hand tenderly and gives me an understanding look. Neither of us says anything for a few moments.

It didn't seem like ten years had passed, she says.

What? I ask. What didn't?

I was just thinking. At the reunion. I thought we'd just be able to pick up where we left off. I thought the same thing at our fifteen and at our twenty. The exact same thing.

Decades—not years, but decades had passed, we were with other people, we had children, entire lives the other didn't know about, and I was thinking the same thing. Part of me still believes it. Isn't that just the most absurd thing you've ever heard?

Not even close. Part of me still believes it too.

Lionel Richie never wrote about this, did he?

I smile. Not as far as I know, but I haven't exactly kept up with him. I didn't even know he had a daughter.

She laughs.

I say, I've had some very serious girlfriends over the years—high school, college, graduate school.

Congratulations!

I smile again. Let me finish. They were actual, intimate long-term relationships, but I'm not hung up on any of them. Only you—and we never even dated.

Maybe that's why. With the others you took the relationship as far as it could go. We never got the chance to do that, were never able to get each other out of our systems.

What might have been is more powerful than what was?

You know what was, but what might have been holds so much promise, we're hung up on unrealized potential.

I think it's more than that.

Me too, but I think that's part of it.

Do you think if we had gotten together, we'd've stayed together?

I do.

Me too, I say. There's nothing that can get you out of my system. Nothing at all.

Taking her hand, I place it over my heart.

Put me as a seal over your heart.
For love is as strong as death.
Its flashes are flashes of fire.
The very flame of God.
Many waters cannot quench love.
Nor rivers overflow it.

That's beautiful, she says. What is it?
Egyptian love poetry from the Bible.
That's something else I like about you.
That I know Egyptian love poetry from the Bible?
She smiles. You're a romantic.
Am I?
And there aren't many of us anymore. And it's one thing to start out as a romantic, but to still be one after the world has pounded on you for forty-something years . . . that's quite another.

I nod, and think about it, but don't say anything.

The door opens and a round older man in a black suit and name tag brings more flowers in.

Carrie returns to examining the expressions of sympathy.

They just keep coming, the rotund man says between labored breaths.

That's great, I reply. Do you need help? Are there others?

This is it for the moment, but I'm sure there'll be more soon.

Thanks for bringing them in.

All part of the service.

I give him a quizzical look he doesn't see, and think, What an odd thing to say.

When he leaves, I turn to rejoin Carrie and find her crying. Withdrawing a tissue from the box on the table beneath the mirror, I hand it to her.

Thanks.

All part of the service.

She laughs, dabbing at the corners of her eyes.

Reaching up and gently touching her face, wiping away a tear with my thumb, I say, I want to know what my life would've been like with you in it.

I am in it.

All the way in it.

Me too.

I've always thought that the real tragedy of life is not that it's so short, but that we only get one.

Maybe we get another go.

Still an optimist, I see.

Well, we might. Some people believe that.

A stanza from the Longfellow poem comes to mind and I say it out loud.

> Tell me not, in mournful numbers,
> Life is but an empty dream!
> For the soul is dead that slumbers,
> And things are not what they seem.

Life is real! Life is earnest!
And the grave is not its goal;
Dust thou art, to dust returnest,
Was not spoken of the soul.

Exactly, she says. That's . . . it exactly.
But do you think we get another shot at this life or
just—
Why not? Reuse, renew, recycle.
God, I'd love to believe that.
Let's do.
My eyes drift over to the casket. I'm not sure I can.
Can you?
Just being here like this with you makes me hopeful.
But who's to say we'd do things any differently?
I am. I know we would.
We are quiet again.
Who's the poet you're always quoting? she asks.
Rumi?
Quote something for me. To me.

In your light I learn how to love.
In your beauty, how to make poems.
You dance inside my chest where no one sees you,
but sometimes I do, and that sight becomes this art.

Oh God. That's so . . . she squints, searching for the
word, so . . . lovely. I see why you're so passionate about
him. He's a kindred soul of yours.
Wow. Thanks. That means more than—

But I have to tell you.

Yes?

I've always liked your stuff better.

That's sweet.

I'm not being sweet. I mean it. Your words are my favorite ever penned—and would be even if I didn't know you. I like your translations. I do. A lot. But your poetry, your prose moves me more than any ever written.

It's just not fair.

What?

This. Life. We're not ready for it when it comes. Can't prepare for it. It comes too fast. It's over too soon. It's like this carnival ride spinning out of control, and we can't stop it. We just hang on and try to survive and we miss so much and then it's over. It's over and we can't get it back. I want a do-over. We should get that. At least one. One time where we can say, hey that thing I missed back there was too important, too vital to my life. I can't miss it. I just can't. And they should let us go back to it. Just once. Just one moment where I turned one way and should've turned another. I didn't know then, but I know now. I could turn the right way this time.

Looking far away, Carrie's next words are soft, said to herself in nearly a trancelike state. We dream our dreams, live our little lives, make our mistakes, and then we're gone.

Gone. . . Forever do you think?

Maybe.

What happened to your optimism?

Death killed it.

Don't let it, I say. What about this? Us?

Exactly.

No. Don't let it end like this. Stop it. I want a happy ending.

There are no happy endings, she says. Just endings.

We are quiet a long time after that.

You doing the eulogy? she asks.

I nod.

You'll do a great job.

I don't know, I say. How do you sum up an entire life in ten minutes?

Maybe you don't even try.

Then what?

Just capture the person you knew. I mean really capture her. Be honest and specific. Share key moments you had with her.

But what about all the moments—key and otherwise—she had with other people.

The other people will remember those, she says. Share your memories and they'll have memories of their own.

I wish you could do it.

I'm glad it's you. You'll do fine. Just fine.

If I forget anything, you could speak up.

No, I don't think I could. But I won't need to. You'll do fine.

I want to so badly, but I don't know.

You will.

Thanks.

I should leave you alone to prepare.

No. Stay. Help me.

Okay, she says, but just for a few more minutes. Tell me what you remember about her.

She was so pretty—so pretty, but she was sweet and smart too. So smart. So sweet.

That's nice, but too generic. Give me a memory. Tell me a story.

The first time I saw her, I fell in love. Her dad was in the Air Force. He was transferred to Tyndall when we were in seventh grade. I remember when the principal brought her to the art room and introduced her to our class. She was dressed so differently from the rest of us—current, hip, stylish. She was a big-city girl coming to the small town. She had this look on her face. Kind of wary, kind of hopeful. It said, Like me. And I did.

That's better, but still doesn't tell us much.

Every guy wanted to date the new girl.

You?

I had a girlfriend at the time. I broke up with her eventually, but not soon enough. By the time I was free . . . Anyway, she was so interesting, had lived all over the world. She knew so much, had experienced so much, yet she really fit in with all us small towners.

She was a chameleon then?

She had to be, I think, but not in a bad way. It didn't seem fake or forced, but like she was selectively exposing different facets of herself. We all do it to a certain extent, don't we? She was just very skilled at it.

She smiles and nods, but doesn't say anything.

Should I tell them I was in love with her, that I've been in love with her, that I'm still in love with her?

I think they'll know. Just make sure they realize she felt the same way.

Breaking down, I say, Oh, God, I can't do this.

Sure you can. What other choice do you have?

I could join her.

But you still haven't figured out the meaning of life.

What if she was it? I ask.

She's not. What you feel for her—what she feels for you—is part of the meaning of life, part of it to be sure, but not all, not all of it.

Right now it feels like all of it.

I know.

You're sure it's not?

Positive, she says.

Still.

Any thoughts on the afterlife?

Nothing profound.

I'd still like to hear them, she says. They're particularly relevant to me at the moment.

Okay. If there's an afterlife, I think it's likely to be an extension of this life.

If?

Sorry, but that's about the best I can do right now.

Isn't my being here proof that there is one?

It certainly seems so. Of course, I could just be delusional, imagining all of this.

She leans in and kisses me. This kiss is gentle, but long and intense. When she pulls back, both of us breathless, she asks, Was that imaginary?

If it was, my imagination is far more developed than

I thought.

It's possible, I guess, but please continue.

I think this life is a sort of boot camp for the next. We prepare, work on ourselves, learn what we can, grow and evolve—and who we are, our core, remains intact somehow.

So we're not made perfect, don't become angels or something?

Right, I say. Sure, we shed some of the things that hold us back—infirmities, addictions, maybe even self-deception, but who we really are remains.

So the way we live this life determines the next?

Yeah, but not in some heaven or hell, reward and punishment way. It has nothing to do with that. It's more . . . missed opportunities.

Opportunities?

Here and now. Every day. The little choices that seem so inconsequential are really determining our fates.

So that's it. Whatever I did or did not do, there's nothing I can do about it now.

Actually, I'm not so sure. I think we'll still have opportunities to grow and become.

What about all the heaven and hell stuff?

Metaphors for the choices we make.

What about God? Doesn't she have something to say about it?

Freedom—our freedom is too important. Think about this life. She never makes us do what's right, nor punishes us when we don't.

That's true.

If there is a God, I say, then he or she loves us unconditionally. What we do with that—abuse it or share it or thrive in it—is up to us. God created us to determine our own destinies.

Brave, that.

Insane, some might say.

I've really got to go now.

No, I say, my voice breaking. Please. No. Not yet.

I have to.

Please. Just a little longer. Please.

I can't, she says. I wish I could. Hey—

I look at her, our eyes holding the moment, even as they fill with tears.

You'll do fine.

Should I tell them about the time we got locked in the school together? How badly I wanted to kiss you, but never worked up the nerve, and how I always regretted that.

I don't just mean with the eulogy. With everything. I'll see you around.

Will you? I ask. Will we be together?

She says, Live like we won't, but believe that we will. Don't put anything off. Don't live like you'll have another chance. But know that you and I will be together one day.

Will we? I ask.

Before she can answer, the door opens and mourners begin to pour in. Turning back to her, I say, See, I told you'd there'd be a good—

But she is gone.

I am alone.

I try to hold it together in front of the others, but am unable.

My eyes sting, my heart sinks, my head hurts, my vision blurs, as an old, familiar anxiety spreads through me like poison shot into my veins, and in this moment I feel more loneliness than I've previously experienced. Ever. I'm not sure I can get up, to rise or speak, let alone go on with the rest of my life—my life without her.

After a while, the small chapel is filled with friends, family, and our old classmates, and I'm simultaneously angry there aren't more here and that they're here at all— that I have to share her in any way, that their arrival induced her departure.

Eventually, I stand and place the story I wrote and brought for her into the open casket where she lays, then step over to the podium beside it and begin her eulogy.

> The minute I heard my first love story,
> I started looking for you, not knowing
> how blind that was. Lovers don't finally meet
> somewhere.
> They're in each other all along.

The mystic poet Rumi wrote those words seven centuries before I met Carrie for the first time and fell in love with her and discovered she had been in me all along. We were thirteen and thought our lives would go on forever . . .

Nine

I can't recall all that is said at the memorial service
or the grave, by me or anyone else, only disjointed phrases,
disembodied words, but nothing clings to my remembrance
the way the hitchhikers did my pant legs during the funeral
processional through the overgrown cemetery quite like the
finality of the minister's final words.

For as much as it has pleased Almighty God to
take out of this world the soul of Carrie Ann Winslow, we
therefore commit her body to the ground, earth to earth,

ashes to ashes, dust to dust, looking for that blessed hope when the Lord Himself shall descend from heaven with a shout, with the voice of the archangel, and with the trump of God, and the dead in Christ shall rise first. Then we which are alive and remain shall be caught up together with them in the clouds to meet the Lord in the air, and so shall we ever be with the Lord, wherefore comfort ye one another with these words.

I find nothing in the words that offers me any comfort, not anything I might use to comfort others. She is dust. I am ash. What comfort is there in that?

First I was raw, then I was cooked, then I was ash.

Ten

Long after Carrie's uncoiled mortality has been laid to rest, long after every other mourner returns to their lives, as if for them life could continue somehow, I return to the chapel hoping beyond all hope and reason I might see her again.

Alone.

I only thought I felt lonely before.

Carrie had been out of my life before—much of it, in fact—but this was the first time even the possibility of her was gone.

I linger a long time in the dim, empty, lifeless chapel that now feels like a body without a soul.

A faint floral scent hangs in the still air as if stuck, overwhelmed occasionally by the sickly strong olfactory fragments of old-lady perfume trapped here since those wearing it left it behind.

She is not here. She does not appear.

Eventually, I whisper her name. Carrie.

There is no response.

Carrie. Please. Please come back.

Please.

Nothing.

She is gone.

Had she ever really been here?

Had I just imagined the whole—wait. If I were deranged, if I had just made up the entire encounter, why wasn't I hallucinating her here with me right now?

I am with you, she says.

It's her voice, but it comes from inside me.

Oh God, I miss you so much, baby. Please don't leave me like this. Please come back. Just for a little while longer. Please.

I'll always be with you. Always. Never doubt that.

Doubt thou the stars are fire;
Doubt that the sun doth move;
Doubt truth to be a liar;
But never doubt I love.

As if ignited by an orange-emblazoned ember,

warmth emanates outward from her words unto my body entire, unto the tip of every extremity, every part, every cell.

But you have things to do. Travel your path. Complete your journey. Don't wait. Start now.

How?

Hafez, she says, and it is the last word I ever hear her say.

Among all the translations of the fourteenth-century Persian poet I've done, one stanza stands out. This is what Carrie's one word meant. This is my work, my path, this moment.

> Don't surrender your loneliness so quickly.
> Let it cut more deep.
> Let it ferment and season you
> as few human or even divine ingredients can.
> Something missing in my heart tonight
> has made my eyes so soft
> my voice so tender
> my need of God
> absolutely clear.

Michael Lister

A native Floridian, award-winning novelist Michael Lister grew up in North Florida near the Gulf of Mexico and the Apalachicola River where most of his books are set.

In the early 90s, Lister became the youngest chaplain within the Florida Department of Corrections—a unique experience that led to his critically acclaimed mystery series featuring prison chaplain John Jordan: POWER IN THE BLOOD, BLOOD OF THE LAMB, FLESH AND BLOOD, THE BODY AND THE BLOOD, and BLOOD SACRIFICE.

Michael won a Florida Book Award for his literary thriller DOUBLE EXPOSURE, a book, according to the *Panama City News Herald*, that "is lyrical and literary, written in a sparse but evocative prose reminiscent of Cormac McCarthy." His other novels include THUNDER BEACH, THE BIG GOODBYE, BUNRT OFFER-INGS, SEPARATION ANXIETY, and THE BIG BEYOND.

Michael's "Meaning" books are meditations on how to have the best life possible and include THE MEANING OF LIFE IN MOVIES, THE MEANING OF JESUS, and MEANING EVERY MOMENT.

www.MichaelLister.com

You buy a book.

We plant a tree.